Enid

# A SUR
# FOR MOLLY

Pictures by Sally Holmes and Ken Stott

**COLLINS COLOUR CUBS**

The children were in the playroom, playing with their toys, when Mummy called to them.

"Alan! Mollie! You really must go out into the garden this nice sunny day! Hurry now!"

"Oh, Mummy – just a minute!" cried Mollie. "I'm putting my doll to bed. She's got measles."

"Well, it would be better to take her out in her pram, a nice day like this," said Mummy, coming into the playroom.

"Mummy, it would be dangerous," said Mollie. "Alan's the doctor, and he told me to keep Angela in bed for two days. Please just let me finish tucking her up."

"Very well," said Mummy. "Then go out and play till I call you in for lunch. And come in with good appetites, please,

because there will be egg-salad – and for a treat you may have a very little cucumber!"

"Ooooh!" said the children. They loved egg-salad, and they thought cucumber was so cool to eat, though they were not allowed very much.

"There will be juicy little tomatoes, too," said Mummy. "So come in as soon as you hear me call."

Mollie finished putting her doll to bed. Angela's bed was a big cardboard box that Mummy had lined for her with some pink padded silk. Mummy had made her a pillow, too, and Mollie herself had made the little sheets and blankets. Angela really looked sweet in the bed.

"Hurry up," said Alan, impatiently. "I want to play Red Indians. You *are* a time, Mollie!"

"I'm ready now," said Mollie, and she stood up. "Goodbye, Angela, dear. I hope you will go to sleep."

The two children went out into the
sunny garden. It was lovely out there. The
sun was warm, the bees were humming,
and the sparrows were chirping madly.

"Now we're Red Indians," said Alan.
"Here's a spear for you. We'll hide in the
bushes and jump out if an enemy comes."

It took them all the morning to play their game, and they were hot, hungry, and tired at the end of it. They were pleased to hear Mummy call.

"Good!" said Alan. "Egg-salad - cucumber – lettuce, and radishes, I expect – and little juicy tomatoes out of the greenhouse. Hurrah!"

They ran in. Mummy called to them from the playroom, where she was busy setting out the lunch. "Wash your hands and do your hair, please."

They were always supposed to do that before a meal, but they always had to be told! Off they went to wash, and then they brushed their hair neatly.

There came a ring at the front-door bell just then. Mummy had to go and see who it was, and then spend a few minutes talking to the caller. The children were impatient, for they were hungry. They waited in the hall for Mummy. At last she shut the front door and came over to them.

"Well, I'm ready at last," she said. "Come along."

They went to the playroom. Mummy
had set the lunch out on the table by the
window. Alan ran over to it. He looked at
the salad.

"Oh, Mummy! You said we could have
some cucumber – and there isn't a single
bit on the dish! And there aren't any
tomatoes either."

"Yes, there are," said Mummy. "I put them there myself!"

But when she came over to the table, too, she stared in surprise. Alan was quite right. There wasn't any cucumber, and not a single tomato either!

Mummy turned the salad over with a spoon. No – there really was only lettuce and radishes. How very queer! Mummy looked at the two children.

"You haven't slipped in here, surely, and eaten the cucumber and tomatoes yourselves?" she asked.

"Of *course* not, Mummy!" cried both children, at once. "You know we wouldn't."

Mummy looked all round the room as if to see who could possibly have taken some of the salad. "It's most extraordinary," she said. "No bird would come and steal the cucumber and the tomatoes – and certainly no cat or dog would. Then who in the world has taken them?"

Alan and Mollie looked all round the room, too, but they couldn't see anyone or anything that might have stolen their salad. But Mollie suddenly noticed something that made her cry out in surprise.

"Who's thrown Angela out of her bed? Look – poor darling, she's lying on the floor, face downwards – and she's ill with the measles, too. Alan – did you do that?"

"No, I didn't," said Alan. "Of course I didn't. Aren't I Angela's doctor? Would I throw a patient out of her bed on to the floor? Don't be silly."

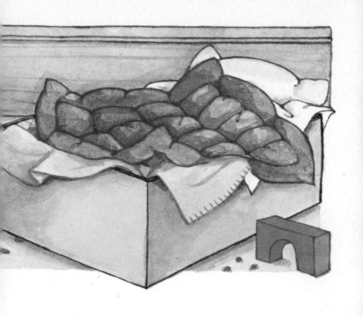

"Well, who did, then?" cried Mollie. She ran over to her doll and picked her up.

"Mollie, you really must come and have lunch now," said Mummy, thinking that Mollie would be a long time tucking her doll up in bed again. "Come along now. You can see to Angela afterwards."

"Oh, Mummy, just let me put her into her bed," said Mollie. She put her hand on the little blankets to pull them back – and then she gave such a squeal that Mummy and Alan almost jumped out of their seats.

"Oooooooooh! There's somebody in my doll's bed! Look! Look! What is it?"

Mummy and Alan ran to see. And whatever do you suppose was lying fast asleep in the little bed? You would never, never guess, I'm sure! It was a small brown monkey, curled up under the sheets, his head on the pillow, fast asleep!

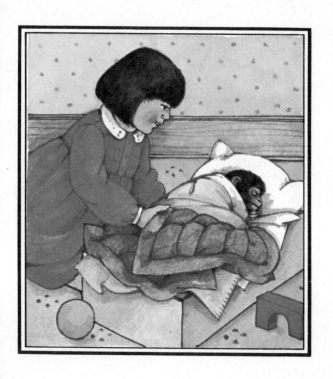

"Is he real?" said Alan. "Yes – he must be. He's breathing. Oh, Mollie – I do think he's rather sweet."

"Why – he must be Major Beeton's pet monkey!" cried Mummy, in the greatest surprise. "I met him this morning, and he

told me the little thing had escaped. You know, he is usually kept in a big cage, and he has a little basket in the cage, with a pillow and blankets that he rolls himself in. That's why he has cuddled down into your doll's bed, Mollie. It reminded him of his own little basket."

"Well, he shouldn't have thrown poor Angela out," said Mollie. "Mummy, doesn't he look funny in my doll's bed?"

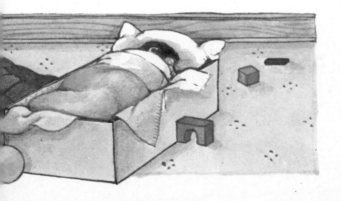

"Mummy, was it the monkey who took our cucumber and tomatoes from the salad?" asked Alan, suddenly. "Do monkeys like them?"

"Of course!" said Mummy. "He must have looked in at the window and seen our nice lunch on the table. And he just helped himself to what he liked the most! Then he wanted to sleep, and found himself a bed."

"I like him," said Alan. "I wish we could keep him. If Mollie didn't want him to sleep in her doll's bed I would let him have my big bicycle basket."

"I expect Major Beeton will want him back," said Mummy. "Shut the window, will you, Alan. And you shut the door, Mollie. Then if he wakes he can't get out. I'll go and telephone to Major Beeton."

Mummy went off to the phone. The children shut the door and the window. Mummy soon came back.

"Major Beeton is delighted that we have found Marmaduke," said Mummy.

"Oh, is that his name?" asked Alan. "Doesn't it suit him, Mummy! Marmaduke, the monkey. It's lovely."

Marmaduke woke up when he heard his name. He sat up in bed and looked at the children and Mummy. Then he jumped out, ran to the table, and climbed up on Mollie's knee. She was so pleased that she could hardly speak.

"Oh, I wish we could keep him," she said. "I do like him so. I love my dolls and my other toys – but they don't run about and climb on my knee like Marmaduke."

Marmaduke behaved himself very well indeed. He took a bit of lettuce from Mollie's plate and nibbled a bit of hard-boiled egg that Alan gave him. He loved the ripe plum that Mummy took from the dish on the playroom dresser, and the children thought he was very clever when he carefully took off the skin before eating it. He was rather rude about the stone, though. He spat it out on the floor.

"He ought to belong to us, really," said Alan, picking up the stone. "We could teach him his manners."

When Major Beeton came to get his monkey the children were sad.

"We do wish we could have him," said Mollie. "You know, Major Beeton, he hasn't got very beautiful manners – but I'm sure he could learn."

"Well, you come and teach him some, then," said Major Beeton. "Come to tea with me each week, and we'll have old Marmaduke out of his cage. You shall play with him and teach him as many manners as you like. But I'm not sure he'll learn them!"

The children were simply delighted. They are going to tea with Marmaduke to-morrow – and what do you think Mollie has got as a present for him? One of her doll's best hats, trimmed with a red feather. Won't Marmaduke look fine!

ISBN 0 00 123735 7
Text © Darrell Waters Ltd
from *Tales After Tea*
Illustrations © William Collins Sons & Co Ltd 1982
Printed in Great Britain